Eat Together

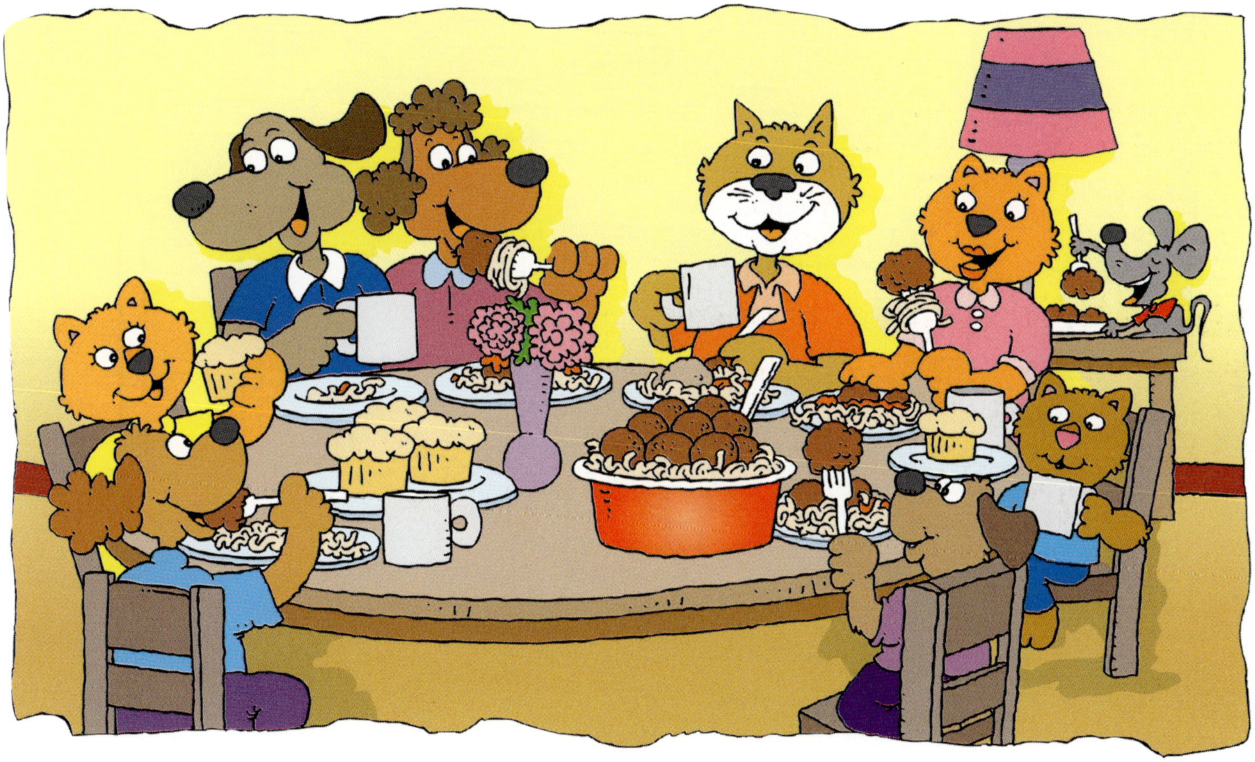

By Carolyn Satoh   Illustrated by Mike Dammer

Target Skill Consonant Mm/m/
High-Frequency Words *a, to*

Scott Foresman
is an imprint of

I am Mom.

I am talking to Mom.

I am mixing the muffins.

I am reading to mouse.

I am eating a muffin.

I am eating a meatball.

I am mopping the mess.